for all the Nanas — stay bad

First published in Great Britain by
HarperCollins *Children's Books* in 2018
Published in this edition in the USA in 2021
HarperCollins *Children's Books* is a division of HarperCollins*Publishers* Ltd,
HarperCollins Publishers
1 London Bridge Street
London SE1 9GF

The HarperCollins website address is:
www.harpercollins.co.uk
1

Text and illustrations copyright © Sophy Henn 2018
All rights reserved.

ISBN 978-0-00-839850-7

Sophy Henn asserts the moral right to be identified
as the author and illustrator of the work.

Typeset in New Clarendon 14/22pt by Goldy Broad
Printed in China

Conditions of Sale
This book is sold subject to the condition that it shall not, by way of trade
or otherwise, be lent, re-sold, hired out or otherwise circulated without the
publisher's prior consent in any form, binding or cover other than that
in which it is published and without a similar condition including this condition
being imposed on the subsequent purchaser.

MIX
Paper from
responsible sources
FSC™ C007454

This book is produced from independently certified FSC™ paper
to ensure responsible forest management.

For more information visit: www.harpercollins.co.uk/green

BAD Nana

OLdeR NoT WiSeR

Sophy Henn

HarperCollins *Children's Books*

CONTENTS

SUPER DUPER

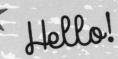

Hello!

My name is
Jeanie
and I am 7 ¾.

I like
buttons, cookies,
and **cats** that play
pianos.

But not **always**
in that order.

I have three very **best friends**. They are called Sukey, Marcy, and Wilf. I like them **all** totally equally so don't **even** ask me who my best friend is (sometimes it's Marcy but not all the time).

I like **almost** everyone except Georgina Farquar-Haha and I don't even really **not** want to like her, but she has made it **impossible** to.

I'M WITH STUPID

I live here with my mom and dad and a whiny noise called Jack. Jack is SUPER annoying. His face is annoying, he smells annoying, his voice is very annoying and everything he says and does is annoying. I don't really know what the point of him is. Except to annoy me. Which he is EXTREMELY good at.

VERY ANNOYING FACE

SUPER-ANNOYING VOICE

DOING ANNOYING THINGS

SMELLS ANNOYING

OVERALL COMPLETELY ANNOYING

Familywise, I also have **three** aunties, six uncles, **eight** cousins, and a lady we call aunty even though she **isn't** really.

Obviously they don't ALL **live** with us since that

would be **ridiculous**. And I would
NEVER get to **choose** what we watched
on TV because I hardly ever do **now**
when there are only
four of us.

Some other relatives that DON'T live with us are my **three grandmas**.

One is called *Shirley* and she's gone to Devon. We haven't seen her in **ages**.

One is called *Granny Rose* and she is
very nearly completely **peach-colored**.
Even her hair. She smells like talc and
flowers, and everything in her house
has a tiny lace mat underneath it.
Cups, vases, china lambs,

plates, bowls of fruits,

EVERYTHING . . .

19

Except for the
toilet paper—
that has
a dress.

I am not even joking.

My other grandma is called

BAD NANA.

Well, that's not her actual, actual name. I can't even remember what that is as we only ever call her BAD NANA and she doesn't even mind. In fact, I think she quite likes it.

BAD NANA is very different from *Granny Rose* and *Shirley*. Her face is quite a lot more pointy and her glasses are enormous. She has jet-black hair that comes out of a bottle, but I haven't a clue how. She wears a BLACK dress, pointy BLACK shoes and gigantic earrings. She says they are for a little bit of twinkle . . .

but I have **no idea** what
that **actually** means.

For someone
on the small side,
BAD NANA has a completely
ginormous
handbag.

She's never EVER without it.
It is black and shiny and
smells like new shoes. I actually
haven't seen **inside** it—I don't
think **anyone** has—apart from
BAD NANA. But based on guesswork
and memory this is what I **think**
is in there . . .

LOVELY BIG BAG OF LEMON DROPS

SPARE SPARKLY SPECS

STINKY FISH PASTE

FOR PINNING

NAIL POLISH

PPFFFFTTTTT!

WHOOPEE

FACE POWDER

SUPER SHARP POINTY TACKS

TROUBLE

YUCK!

COMB/MUSICAL INSTRUMENT

EMERGENCY TEABAG

BUCKEYE

LIPPY

ROGUE LEMON DROP

FOR ANYTHING

FOR NOSE DABBING

FOR LIBERACE

POTENTIAL POCKET MONEY

RAIN HOOD/CATAPULT

KITCHEN SINK
(Dad says it must be in there)

EMERGENCY UNDERWEAR ELASTIC

FOR STICKING

NO IDEA

For back-up or **extra-long** journeys or just shopping she has her even more **humongous** plaid cart. What's inside that is quite a **mystery** and if I'm a hundred per cent truthful I am NOT at all sure I even **want** to know. She also has a walking stick with her at **all** times.

No one is completely sure if BAD NANA actually NEEDS the stick for walking purposes. But we definitely DO know she needs it for tapping TALL people on the shoulder, *reaching* high-up shelves in the supermarket, tripping people up, and waggling it around when she is angry.

On super-special occasions **BAD NANA** pops on her SP$_A$R^{K}LY pink turban. I am not exactly sure why—maybe you need MORE twinkle for special occasions . . . I really don't know as I find I don't really need any twinkle EVER.

But **BAD NANA** says it gives her an air of mystery. Well, if the mystery is WHERE IS THE ALIEN OVERLORD HIDING? then she's SPOT on!

BAD NANA lives at 66 Broadbottom Road, which is exactly eight minutes and thirty-six seconds from my house, if you shake a leg. Or five years if you are Jack and take FOREVER to walk ANYWHERE. He really has NO sense of urgency.

Her house looks a bit like a **toadstool** because it's mainly **roof** and not so much **house**. This seems to be how OLD people like their houses as there are practically hundreds around where **BAD NANA** lives and they **all** have OLD people living in them.

I actually do like **BAD NANA'S** house, though, because you **never** need to wear a sweater, there are **always** cookies, and it **smells** of tea and mischief. It's a good thing I DO like it, because I am around at **BAD NANA'S** house A LOT. My mom works and my dad does too, so they are always busy right up to their **eyeballs**. I am mainly there after school, but sometimes before and sometimes **even** on Saturdays. But NOT Sundays, for Pete's sake.

Unfortunately Jack has to be at **BAD NANA'S** A LOT too, which is very annoying as he ruins everything. I am certain **BAD NANA** feels the same way I do about Jack and wishes he had never been born, but she is very good at hiding it and won't ever admit it, even though I ask her all the time and promise NOT to tell Jack. Which is extremely kind of her when you think about it.

Liberace the cat lives at **BAD NANA'S** house too. Liberace is NOT like any other cat I have ever seen. There are two main reasons for this.

The first is that Liberace is pink. I am almost ninety-eight per cent certain this is **BAD NANA'S** doing as cats are usually ginger or black or white, or black AND white, but almost NEVER pink. **BAD NANA** swears Liberace is completely *entirely* naturally pink, but I strongly feel this is not *quite* the truth as Wilf pinkie-promised he saw Liberace under one of the dryers at *Silveen's Salon* in town. And that's where you go if you want pink or lilac or even mint-green hair.

The other main reason Liberace is unusual is because he looks surprised about EVERYTHING. From the moment he opens his eyes he looks like he is being surprised again and again and AGAIN, like he is never NOT being surprised.

Personally I like surprises, but Liberace doesn't look like he enjoys them at all. Which is a shame, seeing as he seems to have more surprises than anyone I know.

BROADBOTTOM ROAD

People are always popping in at BAD NANA'S and the person that pops in the most is BAD NANA'S very best friend, Cynth. She just lives across the street so it's really handy. They giggle A LOT and although I don't always understand what they are giggling about I am very happy that they do. It's nice to know you can still have fun with your best friends even when you are really

really really

really really

OLD.

Someone who definitely NEVER pops around to **BAD NANA'S** is Mrs. Farquar-Haha. Her name would suggest she is lots of fun, but actually she is the opposite of fun. This is probably why she and **BAD NANA** NEVER agree on anything.

Mrs. Farquar-Haha is very important in ALL the things that happen where we live. She's ALWAYS at every event with a clipboard, looking down her nose at EVERYTHING. I don't really know what started the feud between Mrs. Farquar-Haha and **BAD NANA**, but it pops up every now and again, like when **BAD NANA** snuck diarrhea tablets in Mrs. Farquar-Haha's cart at the store and got Beryl to price-check them on the loudspeaker.

41

Or when Mrs. Farquar-Haha BANNED
BAD NANA from the line-dancing club
for being disruptive in the
freestyle section.

We thought they might have made friends when they were ACCIDENTALLY locked in the town hall the night before the summer fair and ate all the liqueur chocolates from the raffle stand to survive (it was *only* two hours).

Anyway, by the time the janitor got them out they were looking a bit the worse for wear and doing a two-person conga around the hall. But instead of ending the feud it only seemed to make it WORSE.

And it seems the feud has been passed down to me because Georgina Farquar-Haha (Mrs. Farquar-Haha's granddaughter) is a total MEANIE and makes my life really rotten at every chance she gets. Sometimes I feel like I am tiptoeing on eggshells so I don't do anything embarrassing or silly or funny for her to TEASE me about until the end of time.

Wilf and Marcy, and *even* Sukey, say I shouldn't **worry** about her and I really try NOT to, but when someone gets the whole class to call you $Eggy$ for a WHOLE semester for having egg sandwiches ONCE (thanks, Dad) then I really think you can't be too careful.

And, yes, she is lousy at thinking up **nicknames**.

I honestly don't know how she gets away with it.

And I also honestly don't know where
BAD NANA got her name from.

I mean she's
not bad . . .

or bad...

. . . or even BAD.

She's more up-to-no-good.
Or completely EMBARRASSING.
Or a little bit cheeky.

But she's nearly always GOOD FUN. Things always seem to happen when BAD NANA'S around. You never know what's next.

It can be exciting and very often ends in BIG TROUBLE, but usually for BAD NANA because Dad says she should know better.

But I'm very glad she doesn't.

If the sun has got his hat on, **BAD NANA** is always taking us to the park. I think this is because it is free and isn't the television.

BAD NANA always goes straight to "her" bench as she says her sitting-on-the-grass days are long gone. She can't remember sitting on the floor at all after the millennium, but I don't think the two things are even slightly linked.

The Park

Sometimes someone else is sitting on "her" bench, but this isn't a problem as BAD NANA just walks over, points to the plaque on the bench that says "*In loving memory of Bill,*" and wobbles her bottom lip until whoever is sitting there moves. Sometimes she makes me and Jack stand behind her and look sad, just to be sure.

I asked **BAD NANA** if she actually knew *Bill*. She just said that wasn't the point, and anyhow she always gave *Bill*'s plaque a quick polish with her spare hanky whenever she sat there and would I like a lemon drop?

It turned out I would, so that was the end of that.

Once we visited just after the new park keeper started keeping the park. **BAD NANA** was good friends with the old park keeper, Frank, but he had to move to the seaside to be nearer his grandchildren.

Jack pointed out that **BAD NANA** was really lucky as she didn't have to move because she nearly always had her grandchildren with her almost all the time. **BAD NANA** said "*Hmmmmmm,*" in a funny way, which I think meant she feels very lucky to have me almost ALL the time but would rather have Jack almost NONE of the time.

DO NOT LAUGH

DO NOT HAVE FUN

DO NOT EAT LOLLIES

DO NOT LITTE

Anyway, we were all super **excited** as we thought the new park keeper might make some **really** good changes to the park ... like rollercoasters, ice-cream trucks, and *even* a swimming pool.

It turned out he *had* made **billions** of changes, but NONE of them was a **good** one. Each change was a new **RULE** and he had put them on **signs** all over the place.

DO NOT
SMILE

DO NOT
ENJOY THE
PARK ...

... AT
ALL

There were so many NEW RULES that it made you feel fidgety because you would probably accidentally break a rule and then WHO knows what would happen.

DO NOT ENJOY YOURSELF

Everyone in the park seemed really miserable, which I don't think is the point of a park at all. I felt practically certain that this would give BAD NANA the grumps, because if there is one thing BAD NANA is NOT excited about, it's silly, fun-stopping RULES.

DO NOT PLAY GAME

DO NOT MIME

BAD NANA likes nearly everyone to have fun—that's one of my **favorite** things about her. I could see her getting annoyed as she looked around at everyone being all **miserable**, and in such a lovely park too.

DO NOT FEED THE BIRDS

BIRD SEED

DO NOT DO TWIRLING

Then **BAD NANA** popped in a lemon drop, sat on her/*Bill*'s bench, and had a think. This made me **excited** and **nervous** all at once.

...OR WEAR HATS

DO NOT HAVE PICNICS

As soon as **BAD NANA** had crunched the last of her lemon drop, she sprang into ACTION. Well, maybe it was more of a shuffle, but she definitely meant business!

After a jolly good rummage in her humongous handbag, she told me and Jack to keep our eyes out for the SCARY park keeper while she began cheering the place up a bit.

I had no idea what this meant and wasn't at all sure how **BAD NANA'S** lippy was going to help. But I DID know that it had given me a funny wiggly feeling in my tummy and it was NOT an entirely good feeling.

It turns out my tummy was spot on as **BAD NANA'S** "cheering the place up a bit" actually meant crossing out all the "NOT"s on the park signs.

Jack and I got quite a bit **nervous** keeping our eyes out and we were both rather relieved when **BAD NANA** had finished.

BAD NANA was especially pleased with her work and felt all the new park signs were "much more encouraging and generally positive." Everyone else seemed to think so too and got back to having lots of fun

DO NOT DO
TWIRLING

DO NOT
PLAY
GAMES

DO NOT
READ
BOOKS

...OR WEAR
HATS

surprisingly quickly. The park really was very **cheered up** indeed.

We stopped for a bit of a **breather** after all our **rule breaking**/keeping our eyes out, which I was **very** glad about as I find being a bit **naughty** quite **exhausting**. I have NO idea how **BAD NANA** manages so much **mischief** at her age.

DO NOT
ENJOY
YOURSELF

DO NOT FEED
THE BIRDS

Our celebrations didn't last long, though, as apparently the park keeper did NOT want the park cheered up AT ALL. In fact, any sort of cheeriness or fun quite clearly made him very CROSS indeed. He was SO CROSS even his eyes seemed to CROSS. I honestly think I saw smoke coming out of his ears.

He SHOUTED at everyone having fun in the fountain, he BOOMED at all the people enjoying the grass, he YELLED at everyone getting along with the ducks, and he SCREAMED at an old lady who was just sniffing a rose.

All the fun **stopped** super-double-quick-fast, which I thought was a real shame. I am sure Jack would have thought so too, if he had a brain. BAD NANA'S grumps came back and she started making rather LOUD grumpy, humphy noises until she popped in another lemon drop for a think.

The park keeper was stomping around the place,

checking that there was no one still having ANY sort of fun at all, and was stomping up the path toward us, with his chest all puffed out like a pigeon in uniform. Just before he got to the bench I heard the crunch of a lemon drop and a quiet little cackle from BAD NANA, then I saw a lemon drop wrapper float to the ground. It LANDED on the path in front of us.

I was completely SHOCKED as one of **BAD NANA'S** TOP TEN Things of Importance (they are NOT rules—more like firm suggestions) is DON'T DROP LITTER.

But she had just gone and dropped actual litter AND in front of a furious pigeony park keeper. He stomped to a HALT just before the littering candy wrapper, and his eyes NARROWED as he glared at it and then back at **BAD NANA** and then back at the wrapper. It was extremely tense—SO tense Jack and I might have accidentally held hands. It honestly felt like the whole park was holding its breath. I had no idea how **BAD NANA** was going to wiggle out of this one . . .

BAD NANA looked up and I could see she was giving the park keeper THE BIG EYES and the wiggly OLD-LADY smile. I have seen her use these before in particularly tricky situations. They only really work when people don't actually know what she is really like. She then leaned forward as if she was really trying to pick up the wrapper and made a little noise I have never heard her make before. Like a "fumphfff" or a "finffphfff" or something.

By now all eyes were on the park keeper and he knew it. He couldn't make this little old lady, who seemed to be sort of stuck

on a park bench, pick up
her candy wrapper, not with
EVERYONE watching and not with
her looking so sweet and everything,
could he? In a way that somehow made it
crystal clear he did not really want to,
the park keeper bent down to
pick the wrapper up . . .

. . . and quick as a flash **BAD NANA** ducked behind her **massive** handbag and made the LOUDEST, SQUELCHIEST, longest, FARTIEST raspberry noise. Ever.

The park keeper straightened up super-duper fast and his face immediately went BRIGHT red. He started flapping around all over the place and saying over and over, "It WASN'T me—it was the OLD LADY!"

But BAD NANA was very busy looking extremely sweet and a bit vague so no one believed him for a second. Or maybe they just didn't want to believe him on account of him being such a fun-stopping stinker all day. So the whole park was now laughing and laughing and that seemed to make the park keeper **redder** and REDDER and I thought he was actually going to go POP. But he didn't. Instead he did a funny little bunny hop—I don't know why—and then RAN all the way to his shed, shut the door, and stayed there for the rest of the afternoon.

So we all got to **enjoy** the park again
and **everyone** left it as they had found
it and very definitely put **all** their
garbage in the **can** . . .

BAD NANA saw to that!

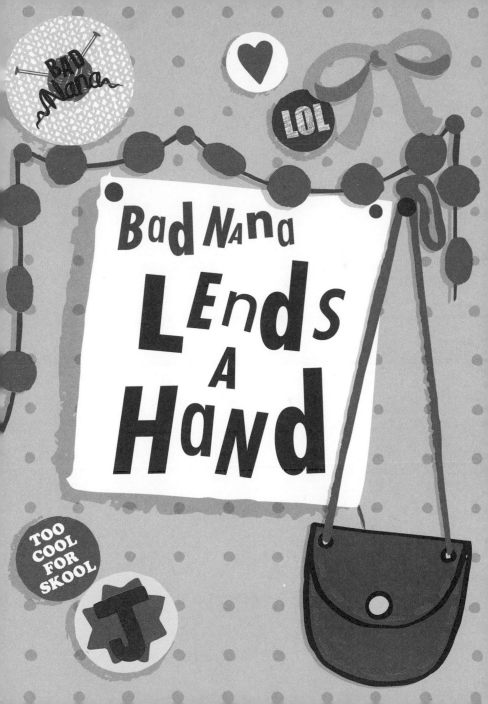

The whole thing started when **BAD NANA** let down the tires on Mr. Pinnock's mobility scooter and everyone agreed she had gone TOO FAR. It didn't matter that Mr. Pinnock had been rude to **BAD NANA'S** best friend, Cynth, in the line at the post office—it was NO EXCUSE!

The next morning, while having a cup of tea with Cynth, **BAD NANA** decided she was done with mischief and she would turn over a new leaf. Cynth and I rolled our eyes at each other—we'd heard it all before. But what we hadn't heard before was that this new leaf meant **BAD NANA** would be volunteering to do "good things for others." Well, this was a completely new leaf altogether. I was confused.

I stopped being confused and started being a bit **fed up** when **BAD NANA** told me her first "good thing for others" involved her helping with the reading at MY school.

I have **enough trouble** with Georgina Farquar-Haha sneaking around the place waiting for me to do something **enormously** embarrassing or just a bit **silly** and then **teasing** me about it FOREVER. Sometimes I don't even know I've done anything out of the ordinary, but Georgina **does** and then she makes **sure** everyone else does too. So having **BAD NANA** around at school the whole time was sure to result in me getting a horrible **new** nickname. And I was just getting comfortable with ODD SOCKS JEANIE. I know, it's a **ridiculous** nickname. Even **more** ridiculous when you consider

my socks

weren't even **odd**—

one had just fallen down.

So I felt ginormously better when it turned out that BAD NANA was "doing good" in Jack's class and helping with reading on Tuesdays and Thursdays.

Once everyone had got the hang of lowering BAD NANA into the tiny chairs outside Cherry Class, she really seemed to be doing a very excellent job of being READING HELPER. It was all going really well and BAD NANA was doing lots of "good things," helping Jack and his class read better. They all seemed to really enjoy reading with BAD NANA and their vocabulary was GROWING in all kinds of NEW and interesting ways.

Things only got into a bit of a pickle when Jack's best friend, Ollie, came back from his turn reading with BAD NANA and told the class he was a "PROPER DIAMOND GEEZER"* and then asked Miss Peabody what it meant. This made Miss Peabody go a greenish-type color and rush out of the room to the reading corner.

It turned out that BAD NANA had been getting Cherry Class to read her library books, and she had just started a particularly good TRUE-CRIME thriller, which Ollie had been reading. Miss Peabody tried to explain that this was NOT entirely appropriate and BAD NANA said she didn't see why as they were much more exciting than the **Hop and Fluff** books and they had lots of new words for the children to learn and that she was saving a fortune on library fines and as they were all based on real-life events it was a bit like history too! But Miss Peabody was quite sure about NOT wanting five-year-olds to read true-crime stories so **BAD NANA** STOPPED being Cherry Class's Reading Helper.

Jack was quite sad about this, but I was completely relieved as I found having **BAD NANA** in school on not only Tuesdays but Thursdays as well was far too nerve-racking.

* "DIAMOND GEEZER" sort of means "good man", but a bit more illegal and shadier.

I was NOT relieved for long. In fact, quite soon I was totally unrelieved as **BAD NANA** happily told me she had volunteered to be a helper on my school trip to *THE LOCAL HISTORY MUSEUM* aka The MOST BORING PLACE EVER. I was so unrelieved I fell over. Actually. For real.

Somehow Miss Peabody hadn't reported **BAD NANA** to the school office after the reading incident so she was still in the clear to be a school-trip helper. I felt this was very sloppy school security, but as it was too late to do anything I tried to look on the bright side . . . **BAD NANA** could be

LOTS of fun, she always had lemon drops, which were very handy for bus trips, and if I was in her group but Georgina Farquar-Haha wasn't then it might NOT be a complete, TOTAL, one hundred per cent disaster. Maybe.

On the day of the school trip I woke up all ajitter. The butterflies in my tummy had great BIG boots on, and I could *barely* manage my second bowl of Choco Pops.

"Pleeeeeease can **BAD NANA** BEHAVE herself," I said to no one in particular, and tried really, really hard NOT to imagine ALL the absolutely embarrassing things she could do.

Well, even I hadn't bargained for **BAD NANA** trying to get a sing-along going on the bus, but thankfully we were all far too miserable for that.

Normally on school trips we are all giddy with excitement for a whole day out of school. Mr. Holmewood usually has to tell us to "calm it DOWN," or we will "PEAK TOO EARLY!" and we never believe him, which is so silly because he is always right.

But today everyone (except for BAD NANA) was pretty quiet on the bus because we had all been here before. Literally. We had all been to *THE LOCAL HISTORY MUSEUM* before, in First Grade. So we knew what a completely happy-zapping day of boredom lay ahead.

I would like to point out that I normally really like museums. They are full of INTERESTING facts that are actually INTERESTING, sometimes even head-poppingly INTERESTING. Plus they have levers and pulleys and buttons AND gift shops with fancy pencils. But the main fact you learn at *THE LOCAL HISTORY MUSEUM* is that we do NOT have a lot of history, locally.

I could overlook that, though, if it wasn't for the man who works at *THE LOCAL HISTORY MUSEUM*. He seems to love the museum but hates anyone who visits it, which is very confusing. He is even angrier than the lady in the candy shop and she is LIVID. This is a mystery to me as how could you even be slightly peeved if you worked in a candy shop all day long? Mom says it's TOO much sugar.

HALF-MOON GLASSES:
perfect for giving
scary stares over

LIVID EYEBROWS

SUPER BAT HEARING

MAD LASER EYES

Well, it's NOT a smiley
MOUTH, is it?

FURIOUS FLARED NOSTRILS:
the bigger they are the more
furious he is. I know.

ANGRY
HUNCHED-UP
SHOULDERS

POINTY
ANGRY
ELBOWS

POCKET FULL
OF LOZENGES:
so all his angry shouting
doesn't give him
a sore throat

IMPATIENT
TAPPY FOOT:
for making you
more nervous

CARDIGAN FOR
EXTRA WARMTH:
as I suspect he is
made of ice

We arrived at the museum and all flopped off the bus. Mr. Holmewood didn't have to say "BE QUIET" once, not even to Emily Bartlett, and she is ALWAYS talking.

Mr. Holmewood looked a bit worried. Then **BAD NANA** started tutting and eye rolling all at once. I thought she might be having one of her "funny turns" and reached for her bag to get her an emergency lemon drop. But as she

swung the bag away and jabbed her bony finger at the museum sign I realized she was NOT having a turn at all but was in actual fact NOT AT ALL HAPPY.

It turns out **BAD NANA** thought we were visiting the LOCAL **MYSTERY** MUSEUM, which doesn't even exist as far as I know. Anyway **BAD NANA** LOVES a mystery. Her favorite program is COZY VILLAGE MURDERS and we are always on the lookout for something SUSPICIOUS. So you can imagine how completely disappointed she was, especially with *THE LOCAL HISTORY MUSEUM* not only being the most boring museum EVER, but having nothing mysterious about it AT ALL. It was a double blow and **BAD NANA** did not look like she was taking it at all well.

Mr. Holmewood put us all into groups and **mine** was mainly great—it had Marcy AND Wilf in it. Sukey was in another group but she was with her mom and Penny Heard so she didn't **really** mind. Susie Stubbs and Clare Coleman were in our group and they are **sort of friends** with Georgia but also sort of NOT (I think they are mainly **scared** of her and I don't think that is really a **good thing** for a friendship) so I wasn't too

worried about **BAD NANA** doing something double embarrassing.

We also had Lydia in our group. Now, I like Lydia. She is really good at reading and can be quite funny, but she mostly walks on tiptoes so it takes AAAAGES to get anywhere, which is no good for a school trip. I started to feel a bit panicky that we wouldn't get everything done even before Mr. Holmewood had handed out the clipboards and worksheets.

We all lined up under the sign:

THE LOCAL HISTORY MUSEUM
Bringing Local History to Life

which was quite funny because it didn't feel very lively at all.

The FURIOUS museum man was already FURIOUS with us for all the things he was sure we were going to do once we got into the museum, e.g. touching things or running around or talking or laughing or breathing or anything that wasn't **STANDING STILL** and **LOOKING/LISTENING**.

We all drooped into the museum like a line of sad zombies. Someone who didn't know us might have thought we were extremely well behaved, but really we were just sad and bored in advance. Lydia tripped up the steps, which I imagine must have been really tricky to navigate on tiptoes, and straight away the FURIOUS museum man barked at her, then gave her such a stinky look that she went all red and her eyes went a bit watery. Wilf and I held her hands hoping it would help. I think it did.

BAD NANA fixed the FURIOUS museum man with her good beady eye and I knew she wasn't going to be taking much more of his nonsense.

The museum tour began and the FURIOUS museum man suddenly started talking like an ANGRY ROBOT, which after about ten minutes sort of makes you sleepy and nervous all at the same time.

After a bit, Freddie made a yipping noise as he had fallen asleep standing up and was having a dream he was a small dog. The FURIOUS museum man shouted

Freddie awake, which, although startling, was actually a good thing as Freddie was dreaming he was being chased by a big dog, hence the yipping.

The FURIOUS museum man then SHOUT-asked Freddie just how was he supposed to *bring history to life* if visitors kept falling asleep? We all considered this for a while and Freddie even started to answer, something about making it more interesting, but Mr. Holmewood stepped in and said we could talk about that later. I got the impression it was one of those questions grown-ups ask, but they don't actually want an answer for.

During the next looooooooooooong lecture the FURIOUS museum man shouted at Georgina for sneezing, Tim for coughing, Sally for hiccupping (which is double awful as Sally said she only got the hiccups because the FURIOUS museum man made her SO nervous) and Sukey's mom for fidgeting.

Then he made a HUGE shouty mistake by YELLING at BAD NANA for sucking too loudly on a lemon drop and even suggested she had surely had enough lemon drops already.

Well, that was it. BAD NANA'S good beady eye NARROWED and she went a very bright shade of purpley red, which I had never seen her go before. I mean I have seen her go pink, I've seen her go reddish, even red, but I have never seen

the purpley red and I could only imagine
this was NOT A GOOD THING.

FINALLY the lecture stopped and we were given **worksheets**. Mr. Holmewood looked confused when we all grabbed them happily, that had **never** happened before. Anything was better than listening to the FURIOUS museum man talking about the almost **non-existent** local history in his ANGRY ROBOT voice.

As I took my clipboard from Mr. Holmewood, Georgina gave me one of those "I'm watching YOU, **Odd Socks**" looks and I tried to make sure I was being completely **normal** and in no way doing anything that looked **odd** or different or tease-able.

I was concentrating **so** hard on this that I **accidentally** walked into a stand with a reproduction **vase** that the FURIOUS museum man thought might have been a bit like the one they had in the museum a **million** years ago when it was actually a house.

The vase wibbled, and then it wobbled, and it wibbled a bit more and then it fell down. The FURIOUS museum man dived and tried to catch the vase, but

he was miles away and actually, it just looked like he fell over all of a sudden. But **Billy** caught it instead as he was right there and an excellent goalkeeper on our school

soccer

team.

Phew! I thought, but then I thought **again** as the FURIOUS museum man got up, dusted himself down, and then started yelling at me so SUPER-DUPER **loudly** I couldn't quite make out what he was saying. It all just *blurred* into one long FOGHORN-TYPE noise. But I did get the impression that what he was saying **wasn't** at all **good**. I am not sure how long this would have gone on for had **BAD NANA** not inserted herself between me and the FURIOUS museum man and told him in no uncertain terms that "accidents happen," there was "no harm done" and that "THAT was quite enough of that." The FURIOUS museum man gave **BAD NANA** a funny look, like he had just swallowed some super-hot chilli sauce, but **BAD NANA** didn't even blink, and off he stomped.

AAAA

I felt a little bit **wobbly**, like I had been in a *WIND TUNNEL* turned to MAX, but **BAD NANA** snuck each of us a lemon drop, for medicinal purposes, and we were off. Everyone was **bobbing** around trying

to be the **first** group to **finish**. It turns out Lydia has got quite fast on her tiptoes, what with mainly walking on them and everything, so we were doing **really** well, until . . .

We were all shuffling past the pretend old bedroom in a sort of SAD conga line. There were fancy ropes that stopped us actually going into the pretend old bedroom, which were quite a bit fancier than the actual bedroom, if I am really honest.

Georgina was right in front of us and telling (boring) the rest of her group about her upcoming dance showcase with Glitter Bugz, the dance group she belongs to. I am not sure it is strictly dancing as it looks more like ELECTRIC SHOCKS and flinging yourself around the place to me.

But I have to say the way they make their **hair** stay straight up and **not** move **one inch**, no matter how much they **fling** themselves and **jump** around, is actually **very impressive**.

Glitter Bugz

Anyway Georgina was explaining a particularly tricky part of their DISCO routine and no one knew (cared) what she was talking about so, with a hairflick/eye-roll combo that quite clearly said we were all idiots, she demonstrated the move.

It was really extremely energetic and so SUPER FAST I couldn't tell you exactly which body part she moved. But what I do know is that the body part hit

Lydia, whose balance was already off, what with her being on tiptoes, so she went *flying* with such DISCO force that the red ropes didn't stop her going into the pretend old bedroom at all. All I heard was a FLUMPHF and a cloud of dust flew up from the bed, and all we could see were Lydia's toes, still pointed, hanging over the end of the pretend old bed.

We all stood super still, like Freeze Tag professionals, then Mr. Holmewood rushed forward to rescue Lydia from the dust, which was settling back down all over her. He needn't have bothered because the FURIOUS man's bellowing unsettled the dust all over again. To say he was FURIOUS was like saying I only like egg sandwiches when I actually LOVE egg sandwiches (even if I can only eat them in the safety of my own home now). He was now definitely infinity FURIOUS. Even Mr. Holmewood looked paler than usual as he stood behind Lydia while the FURIOUS man SHOUTED at her. But then that could have been the dust.

Lydia had gone all **red** again and her eyes were **watering** too and it was all so super **unfair** because it wasn't even her fault, but the **real** culprit, DISCO-**dancing** Georgina, had shimmied away when the yelling started.

When I looked at **BAD NANA** I could see she was that purpley-red color again and I could hardly even see her good beady eye it was so narrowed.

Lunchtime **should** have been **fun**, what with **comparing** packed lunches, **swapping** snacks, and **eating** on the grass, but it WASN'T. Lydia's eyes were still watery and this wasn't helped by Georgina making **snoring** noises and asking her if it was bedtime as she slunk by with her group.

I knew Georgina was a total **meanie**

but I didn't expect her to cause a **complete catastrophe**, not EVEN own up, and then tease the person she'd inflicted the complete catastrophe upon. This was a new low, even for her.

We slowly and bravely ate our sandwiches, chips, cookies, and healthy fruit snacks as **BAD NANA** pointed out we would need our strength for the rest of the visit. We all nodded sadly.

After lunch, we gathered in the Great Hall (it WASN'T great but it was a hall) and the FURIOUS museum man yelled at us about how AAAAGES ago some fancy people would have dinner in this actual room. Apparently some people even thought an old round king had popped by for a feast and eaten LOADS. That's not EXACTLY how the FURIOUS museum man said it, but that's basically what he meant.

Then he said we had to draw an olden-days feast, just like the one they had

set up in the Great Hall using some slightly frightening-looking mannequins, an old wooden table, and some dusty papier-mâché food. I thought it looked a bit like Christmas at Aunty Sandra's house, minus the paper hats.

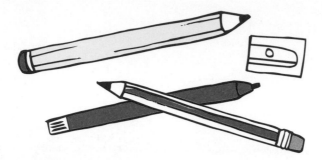

As we all sat down in total silence and started to draw, the FURIOUS museum man marched around and said absolutely NOTHING nice about anyone's pictures.

Then he stopped by Lydia, whose eyes had only just stopped watering, and he looked at her picture. Then, for the first time all day, he smiled. I nearly fell straight over—maybe he wasn't completely FURIOUS after all, maybe he was actually slightly NOT horrible, maybe . . .

But then his smile turned into a creepy sneer and the creepy sneer turned into a NASTY laugh and then the FURIOUS museum man was nastily laughing and creepily sneering and even EVILLY pointing at poor Lydia's drawing. If I am going to be one hundred per cent totally honest, drawing isn't Lydia's best skill, but you can't be good at everything and she is REALLY good at reading and, anyway, I thought it looked a lot like an olden-times feast, sort of.

Georgina, who is never one to miss out on a bit of picking-on-innocent-people-

just-minding-their-own-business, h^opped over and looked at Lydia's drawing and started NASTILY laughing too, which was double annoying as she was the one who had got Lydia into trouble earlier.

Then everyone else started to laugh because if Georgina is laughing and she's not laughing at you, then you'd better join in or else.

With all the NASTY laughing and creepy sneering and EVIL pointing, it wasn't at all surprising that Lydia's eyes started to water and water and she went all pink and looked very wobbly, even though she was sitting down and not even on tiptoes.

I looked around for BAD NANA because I knew she wouldn't be having any of this nonsense, but as I turned around all I could see was her back disappearing behind a curtain. WHAT? Where was she hobbling off to when her group needed her? It was not at all like BAD NANA to shy away from trouble.

I was completely confused and all the LOUD laughing wasn't helping. It was all so unfair and I just couldn't let Lydia and her tiptoes down. Then I realized I had to do something because it really didn't look like anyone else was going to.

I stood up, and I wibbled around a bit because I wasn't **really** sure what I was going to do next and my tummy was doing all kinds of gymnastics and I started to say "STOP!" but it sounded more like a "Squwark!" because my throat was all tight and I looked at Wilf and he was mouthing "WHAT ARE YOU DOING?" at me and I mouthed back "I DON'T KNOW!" while shrugging my

shoulders for extra emphasis, and then I looked at Lydia with her pink and watery face and I tried again . . .

"STOP IT!" I shouted. This time my throat let the actual words out and everyone but the FURIOUS museum man STOPPED. I think they were all a bit surprised because I am not really the shouting type. Then I shouted again "STOP IT, please." (Because manners are still important even if you are talking to a completely mean FURIOUS museum man.) "YOU are just being horrible and mean and NASTY and horrible and . . ."

By this point I realized that he had stopped laughing and the smiley sneer had been replaced by a FURIOUS face, which funnily enough looked almost exactly the SAME as one of the stone gargoyles he had been going on about earlier.

I was a bit stuck then because my brain decided to stop thinking entirely and I just stood there like a total twit with my mouth hanging open and no idea what to do next. This was quite a worry as I could feel the FURIOUS museum man was about to say something and I felt, very strongly, that what he was going to say was NOT going to work out too well for me.

"YOUNG LADY . . ."

he boomed, and although this was a promising start, and not totally insulting, I was very sure it was going to get worse . . .

"WHEN YOU ARE IN MY MUSEUM, *THE LOCAL HISTORY MUSEUM Bringing Local History to Life*, I THINK YOU WILL FIND THAT I CAN DO JUST ABOUT WHATEVER I PLEASE AND FURTHERMORE . . ."

Well, we never did get any further or hear any more because just then a dusty papier-mâché chicken drumstick hit the FURIOUS museum man on the side of his head. Then a dusty papier-mâché apple came flying over and "missed" him

and got Georgina on the forehead. We all turned around to see **where** these things were coming from and saw that history had **actually** really **truly** come to life.

AMAZINGLY the round king in the display was chuckling away merrily

and **hurling** all kinds of papier-mâché food around, but mainly in the direction of the FURIOUS museum man, who was now **more FURIOUS** than ever. But hardly anyone really **noticed** as they were all **dancing** around in front of the display, enjoying *Local History Being Brought To Life* by the round, chuckling king.

Everyone started asking the round king lots of questions because it's not very often you can quiz a sixteenth-century king, chuckling or not. I wanted to ask the round king why all of a sudden he was wearing ginormous glasses and earrings that gave him a little bit of twinkle, but I decided not to as everyone was enjoying themselves too much.

I am not sure all the answers the round king gave were strictly correct, and Mr. Holmewood had to help him out with a few, but all in all I think everyone got something out of it. Even the FURIOUS museum man, because he got THE SULKS.

Big time.

When it was time to go and we were all lining up, the SULKY museum man announced **very** loudly that our school would no longer be welcome at *THE LOCAL HISTORY MUSEUM—*
No Longer Bringing History to Life
because we **clearly** didn't **appreciate** our local history and I thought that was odd

because after the round king came to life it seemed like **absolutely** everyone in my class appreciated history quite a LOT (except for Brian Hargreaves, but then he is only interested in OUTER SPACE and gummy bears). I thought I saw Mr. Holmewood do a little smile when he heard this and maybe high-five the bus driver, but I might have been mistaken. (I WASN'T.)

EXIT
(and don't come back)

BAD NANA came tottering up to the bus at quite a *PACE* for her. She was all out of breath and looked rather warm, which might have had something to do with the red beard she was sporting. Wilf and Lydia and Susie and Clare all ran up to her, yelping about everything that had just happened and asking where she was and wasn't it a shame she missed all the fun? Very hilariously, they didn't seem to notice the beard at all, which I thought spoke very poorly of their image of BAD NANA. We were all in total fits about the chuckling round king and the *flying* papier-mâché food and Georgina's apple in the face and the FURIOUS museum man's sulks.

On the bus on the way home, after I had signaled to **BAD NANA** to remove her beard, I thought about all the future classes who would no longer have to visit *THE LOCAL HISTORY MUSEUM– Definitely Not Bringing History to Life*, and how I had played a small part in that, and how **BAD NANA** had played a big part in that, and how Georgina was now calling me Jeanie Parrot Pants on account of my SQUAWK. Which just goes to show three things . . .

1. Georgina will give me super-awful nicknames no matter what I do so I really can't be worrying about all that. Well, not too much anyway.

And 2. There is a small chance that I will be regarded as a tiny bit of a hero by future students at my school who will not have to visit the most boring and FURIOUS museum in the world, ever. Maybe there would even be a plaque in my honor.

And 3. That while BAD NANA may have been a little bit naughty and maybe even a tiny bit embarrassing, she is mainly awesome.

WATCH Out...
MORE
BAD
Nana
COMING
SOON...